A Panda Bear's Board Game

To order additional copies of this book, contact:
Xlibris
1-888-795-4274
www.Xlibris.com
Orders@Xlibris.com

ISBN: Softcover   978-1-9845-8340-6
         Hardcover   978-1-9845-8341-3
         EBook   978-1-9845-8339-0

Print information available on the last page

Rev. date: 07/24/2020

A Panda Bear's Board Game

Michelle Sheree Andrews

In the school of hard-knocks exist two rival groups of panda bears, the Red Panda Bears and the Panda Bears. Assembly time was the only time they would gather to compete for the prize. Some of the Panda Bears did not have to work that hard to compete, while some struggled to bring forth their talents. A majority of the Red Panda Bears and Panda Bears were dirt-poor and challenged each other to a grammatical game of laughter, considering themselves to be smarter. Others were bullies who cheated to win.

In the city of "A" lived a very shy but covert Panda Bear, Baby Bird Budget that has talents. With starry eyes, Baby Bird Budget was determined to be the smartest board-game maker. "I can do it! I can do it! I know I can do it!" She patted herself on the top of her head and hugged herself tightly until tears filled her eyes.

On her long journey, to improve her board game, she whimpers and cries.Baby Bird Budget recollects that she was so nervous that her presentation did not pass at school. Not a student saw her board game. Too, she remembers how a heckler almost got her laughed out of ABC Elementary School.

But her wise grandfather, Duke of Budget, was someone she dearly loved. In the near future, he would introduce her to the most intelligent Panda Bears in the world, the Counts. Their tasks were to tell young Baby Bird Budget short stories to help her improve her thinking skills and improve her board game, *Panda Bears Checkers*, or lose the game for a lifetime.

In the time being, there lived a cruel ruler that the Panda Bears and Red Panda Bears had gossiped about. They dare not let him inspect their new inventions for approval.

***

In a classroom setting at ABC Elementary School, all the Panda Bears were laughing and bragging about their new toys that had surpassed average. Mack, a Red Panda Bear, told his A-list friends, "My new car just blew all the other cars out of the water." He had ranked in first place at ABC Elementary School.

Mack saw Baby Bird Budget leaving the classroom. He made fun of her. "Hey, Baby Bird Fruitcake, can you at least make a board game and tell us how it works?" Besides, the ruler of the land dare not look at your befuddled strategy.

Tears suddenly filled Baby Bird Budget's eyes. She began to cry louder and louder. Mack and his friends slapped each other high fives and ran in different directions.

Baby Bird Budget's sister, Wu Budget, could hear her crying hysterically from across the yard. She ran across the schoolyard and asked her, "What happened?"

Baby Bird Budget, now sobbing, repeated "they…they called me a "Fruitcake" and said that I cannot make a board game or explain how it works."

"Did the Red Panda Bears embarrass you in front of all the students?"

"Yes," said Baby Bird Budget, "and they all started laughing."

"Do you want them to stop teasing you?" asked Wu Budget.

Baby Bird Budget nodded her head. "Yes."

Wu Budget saw Mrs. Albright, the teacher, locking up her classroom door and grabbed Baby Bird Budget by the hand. Both Panda Bears ran over to Mrs. Albright.

"Mrs. Albright, may we please speak to you for a moment?"

"Why sure, I have time," said Mrs. Albright.

Wu Budget explained, "My sister, Baby Bird Budget, was so nervous that when it was time for her to give her presentation, she said she could not talk. And she walked back to her seat. She was trembling."

"Some of my students do get nervous," said Mrs. Albright.

Wu Budget reached into her sister's bag and pulled out a very colorful board game.

Mrs. Albright examined the board game closely and grinned. "This game has a lot of potential. Take your time, Baby Bird Budget, and improve your game. I will be happy to let you re-enter it in next month's competition, which I do for most of my students. By the way, how long will it take to play your board game?"

"At least twelve hours," said Baby Bird Budget.

Baby Bird Budget then wiped the tears from her eyes and smiled.

Wu Budget told her, "Mama Budget is going to send you over to Grandpa, Duke of Budget. He will help you to overcome your shyness, rebuild your thinking skills, and win this challenge. Grandpa helped me at a young age. You are a very smart student, and if you place in the competition, you can teach that bully Mack a lesson."

Baby Bird Budget could not wait to get home and tell her parents the good news. She told her mom, "I have a wonderful idea for my board game. And if I improve it, I am sure it will win." Baby Bird Budget then hugged herself tightly, and tears filled her eyes again.

Mama Budget put her hand on Baby Bird Budget's shoulder and looked in her daughter's watery eyes. "I already received a phone call from the school proctor. Is it Mack and his friends again?"

"Yes, Mom."

Her mother reached into her purse and gave her a hanky. Baby Bird Budget wiped the tears from her eyes and blew her nose unusually loud, like the sound of a trumpet, like she always did after she cried.

"Now, I want you to listen very closely to me. Your wise grandfather, Duke of Budget, has received reports from the school and me that you are not able to complete any of your presentations. He has already seen your board game, and he is willing to help you overcome your shyness, rebuild your thinking skills, and be an exceptionally good board-game maker." Mama Budget then hugged her daughter and crossed her fingers in hopes that she would be just as high as an achiever as her sister, Wu Budget.

The next day, Baby Bird Budget, arrived at her grandpa's home. She peeked around the door. Duke of Budget was reading the newspaper as usual.

"All right, Baby Bird Budget. I see you. Come on in." Duke of Budget wore wide, bifocal glasses. He leaned forward and stared at her for a moment. "All right, let me see your board game again, my little baby bear."

Baby Bird Budget looked at Duke of Budget with her starry eyes. She reached into her big bag and pulled out her colorful board game.

Duke of Budget took the board game and placed it on the table. "Baby Bird Budget, my funniest baby bear, look me in the eyes and tell me how you discovered the game and how you play it."

When Baby Bird Budget began to speak, she suddenly forgot what to say. Again, her eyes swelled up with tears.

"All right, my little baby bear. I want you to exhale and inhale three times before you begin to speak. Every time you feel nervous, stop, inhale, and exhale and then begin to speak."

Before her presentation, Baby Bird Budget said, "I can do it! I can do it! I know I can do it!" She inhaled and exhaled three times and began to speak. "I compared all the baby bears in the world, and the cutest baby bear is the Panda Bear. I saw a real Red Panda Bear on the internet television. I figured my board game would be a good game to build the Red Panda Bear versus the Panda Bear.

"The object of the board game is to be the first player to get your giant Panda Bears home to foreign territory or the first player to get the Red Panda Bear home to US territory. I had the Red Panda Bear set up in six foreign zoos to come home to the United States. The game takes at least twelve hours to play.

"The giant Panda Bear resides in all eleven zoos: Tennessee, Mexico City, Washington, DC, San Diego, and Georgia. Panda Bear wanted a zoo that would be built in the future in one of the states. The other six zoos are in foreign territory: Europe, Australia, Taiwan, Beijing, Thailand, and Kobe, Japan."

Duke of Budget then applauded. "Your presentation will improve after you meet all eleven of the Counts that reside in these zoos and they tell you short stories. I do believe you will win each challenge."

"I would love to travel to those zoos and meet the Counts," said Baby Bird Budget. Again, her eyes swelled up with tears. She practiced inhaling and exhaling.

Duke of Budget began to speak. "Now, here is the plan. We are going to travel the country and meet intelligent Counts that graduated from the ABC Elementary School with honors. Their job is to tell you a short story. If you improve the board game, it is your board game, and you get to meet the next Count. If you lose the challenge, we will have to take the board game back home, and you are to set the board game aside for a lifetime. And guess what, my dear granddaughter, Baby Bird Budget?"

"Yes, Grandpa?"

"I do believe you are an extremely high achiever."

Baby Bird Budget then said to herself, "I will put on my thinking cap and make the family proud of me." Her eyes swelled up with tears. She patted herself on top of her head twice and wiped the tears from her eyes as she walked home.

The next day, Duke of Budget called all eleven Counts and informed them that he had a winner and he wanted them to use the short-story, guessing game to help Baby Bird Budget improve her board game. "If she guesses right, we will travel and meet the next Count. If she guesses wrong, we will return home, place the board game aside for a lifetime, and make her build another board game."

They all agreed.

He now called Baby Bird Budget's parents and told them that they were definitely going. The Counts agreed to tell her eleven stories to help improve her board game. Mama and Papa Budget were so excited for Baby Bird Budget that Mama Budget prepared plenty of vanilla, strawberry, chocolate, banana, grape, and orange bamboo sticks and thank-you cards to take with her on the trip. Baby Bird Budget packed her clothes and board game inside of a bag.

Duke of Budget told her, "Make sure you pack twelve colored pens, a notepad, and your Giant Panda Bear and Red Panda dice."

Excited about the trip, Baby Bird Budget took her bag, kissed her parent's goodbye, and ran over to Duke of Budget's home. Out of breath, she was now panting heavily, and again her eyes swelled up with tears. She now assured herself that if she put on her thinking cap and inhaled and exhaled three times, she would be able to master every challenge.

"Ready for the trip, my young baby bear?"

"Yes, Grandpa, I am ready!"

Mama and Papa Budget called Duke of Budget and asked him if Baby Bird Budget agreed to take the trip or if she were nervous.

She strongly said, "I am ready."

The parents bumped each other, slapped each other high fives, and hoped that Baby Bird Budget, their youngest daughter, would be able to solve what they figured to be ridiculously sounding riddles.

Duke of Budget studied the map and sets his compass to go to Tennessee.

Overwhelmed with excitement, Baby Bird Budget's emotions were racing so fast that she began to sing to her grandfather, "I love you, and I need you."

Duke of Budget begins to sing "I love you. I love you."

Baby Budget hugged Duke of Budget for his support. They joined their voices together singing, "I love you. I love you."

Traveling for a distance, they finally reached the zoo named Tennessee. There, the Count known as the Mathematician was housed. Duke of Budget now knocked on the Count's door three times.

The Count opened the door and said, "Surprise, surprise, surprise. Come right on in and recline on my grassy couch." He grinned and introduced himself. "Hello, Baby Bird Budget, I am the Count known as Mathematician."

Baby Bird Budget became nervous, and her eyes swelled with tears. He now handed Duke of Budget the script. After reading the script, Duke of Budget now looked at the Count and winked.

Duke of Budget said, "If she answers correctly or comes close to the answer, we win."

"How close?" said the Count.

Duke of Budget said, "Oh, I'll say about 275 points."

"You do not think I like your little granddaughter."

Grandpa again winked.

The Count said, "If your granddaughter does not make the connections, I win."

Again, Duke of Budget winked and told Baby Bird Budget, "Inhale and exhale three times before you answer. Listen very closely as the Count tells you the story."

Baby Bird Budget inhaled and exhaled three times. "I can do it! I can do it! I know I can do it!" She patted herself on the top of her head and hugged herself tightly until her eyes filled with tears.

The Count began to tell his story. "You have a very lovely board game. The Giant Panda Bear and the Red Panda Bear enjoy traveling across the board to get home. There are three rows on each side of your board game, and one square named Enter for each section separating this section from the middle of the board game. The middle section has twenty-nine squares going up and down the board and twenty-nine squares going across. How many squares are on your board game?"

Baby Bird Budget took out her notepad and pen and studied her board game. "I have one column of 24 squares on each side of the board game. I added two more columns.

That is a total of three columns on each side. Seventy-two times two is one hundred and forty-four for two sides of the board game.

"I would like to position the squares on all four sides. One hundred forty-four times two is two hundred eighty-eight squares all around. The middle section has twenty-nines squares up and down the board game and twenty-nine squares across the board game. The middle section equates to twenty-nine times twenty-nine, or eight hundred and forty-one squares.

"One square on top of the first section in each row named Enter separates the middle section of the board game from the first section. A total of six squares named Enter are on each side. Six times two is twelve squares. Six times four squares are twenty-four squares named Enter for all four sides. Two squares vertically separate each row. Four times six is twenty-four. And twenty-four times four is ninety-six. Four squares are beneath each section. Four times six is twenty-four, and twenty-four times four is ninety-six. A sum of 841,288, 24, 96, 96 is 1,345 squares."

The Count said, "The square count is correct. The answer is 1,345 squares. Now, let me see if you made the connections."

The Count almost passed out when he studied her drawing and found out she connected the middle section, the first row, the second row, and the third row.

Duke of Budget told him, "My granddaughter has won the challenge." Then he looked at Baby Bird Budget and said, "Show me what you have drawn that equals 1,345 squares."

Baby Bird Budget showed Duke of Budget how she improved the board game.

Duke of Budget placed his hand over his heart and said, "Highly creative. Good job. Ask the Count to give you a letter of recommendation and give him your vanilla-colored pen."

After he signed, she gave him a vanilla bamboo stick and a thank-you card. Duke of Budget studied the map and set his compass to go to the zoo named Mexico City.

In route to Mexico City, Baby Bear Budget, very elated and full of surprises, began to sing a favorite verse from a song she created. "The rainbow appears after raining makes me proud, and sunshine everywhere makes me happy."

Duke of Budget now joined in and began to sing, "you are my sunshine and will always be mine."

Traveling for a distance, they finally reached the zoo named Mexico City. There the Count known as Artist was housed. Duke of Budget knocked on the Count's door three times.

The Count opened the door and said, "Buenos Dias, my friends. Come right in and recline on my grassy couch." He grinned and introduced himself. "Hello, Baby Bird Budget, I am the Count known as Artist." He studied the improved board game and handed Duke of Budget the script.

After reading the script, Duke of Budget looked at the Count and winked. "If she answers correctly or comes close to the answer, we win."

The Count answered, "How close?"

Duke of Budget wrote down the answer and showed only the Count the answer. They both agreed. Duke of Budget winked.

Duke of Budget told Baby Bird Budget, "Inhale and exhale three times before you answer. Listen very closely as the Count tells you the story."

Baby Bird Budget inhaled and exhaled three times. "I can do it! I can do it! I know I can do it!" She patted herself on the top of her head and hugged herself tightly until her eyes filled with tears.

The Count began to tell his story. "Close your eyes and picture yourself at the top of the mountain with your Panda Bear friends. You have two teams: a team on one side of the board game and a team on the other side of the board game. Which two animals would you choose? Do you see them on your board game? How many animals are on each side of the board game? Place in the middle section one character representing each zoo. Remember to use your rows."

"Starting from left to the right on the side of the board game that starts with Tennessee, I will draw 12 of my Panda Bear Friends in the middle column and a total of 12 Red Panda Bears on the Bottom column. 24 times 4 is a total of 96 Black Panda Bears and Red Panda Bears on all four sides of the board game. In the middle section a Panda Bear is three spaces above each state and territory. Thank you. I think I have figured out a wonderful way to play my board game. "My answer is a sum of 96, 24 and 24 or 144 Panda Bears and Red Panda Bears."

The Count studied the new improved board game. He scratched his head and told her "The correct answer is no less than 60 Panda Bears and Red Panda Bears and no more than 150 Panda Bears and Red Panda Bears. You answered correctly. Good job."

Duke of Budget stared at Baby Bird Budget and asked her, "Show me what you have drawn."

Baby Bird Budget showed Duke of Budget how she had improved the board game.

"Excellent job! Ask the Count to give you a letter of recommendation and give him your strawberry pen."

After the Count signed, she gave him a strawberry bamboo stick and a thank-you card.

Duke of Budget studied the map and set his compass to go to Washington, DC.

Baby Bird Budget, still hopeful and satisfied with her wins so far, began to sing, "If you are happy, say it. If you are happy, say it. If you are happy, say it."

Duke of Budget joined in and begin to sing "and we will be very happy. Clap-clap."

Traveling for a distance, they finally reached the zoo named Washington, DC. There, the Count known as Genius was housed. Duke of Budget knocked on the Count's door three times.

The Count known as Genius opened the door and said, "How are you today, my friends? Come right in and recline on my grassy couch." He grinned and introduced himself. "Hello, Baby Bird Budget, I am the Count known as Genius." He now handed Duke of Budget the script.

Duke of Budget shook his hand. Duke of Budget told Baby Bird Budget, "Inhale and exhale three times before you answer. Listen very closely as the Count tells you the story."

Baby Bird Budget inhaled and exhaled three times. "I can do it! I can do it! I know I can do it!" She patted herself on the top of her head and hugged herself tightly until tears filled her eyes.

The Count began to tell his story. "The Panda Bear went to the store and bought a board game. On the board game, the giant Panda Bear and the Red Panda Bear are located here. Every year people come and visit the Panda Bears and all the other animals. Where do they go? That is what I want you to name your first row. On most board games, all players place their tokens here to begin the game. This is what I want you to name your second row. After leaving the store, she takes her board game, a few groceries, and her mother's change. Where does she go? That is what I want you to name the third row."

Baby Bird Budget wrote her answers down on her notepad in this order. "The first row is named Zoo. The second row is named Start. The third row is Home." She had now improved her board game.

The Count looked at her board game and told her "It is perfect."

Duke of Budget told her, "Ask the Count to give you a letter of recommendation and give him your chocolate pen."

After the Count signed, she gave him a chocolate bamboo stick and a thank-you card.

Duke of Budget studied the map and set his compass to go to San Diego, California. Traveling for a distance, they finally reached the zoo named San Diego, California. There, the Count known as Captain was housed.

Baby Bird Budget began to sing aloud, "I am the little lamb. Grandpa is the bigger lamb. I am the little lamb. Our hair is white as snow." Worried, she now hugged her grandfather for encouragement.

He told her, "Everything will be all right."

Duke of Budget knocked on the Count's door three times. The Count known as Captain opened the door and said, "Welcome aboard, my friends. Come right in and recline on my grassy couch." He grinned and introduced himself. "Hello, Baby Bird Budget. I am the Count known as Captain."

Baby Bird Budget giggled. The Count now handed Duke of Budget the script.

After reading the script, Duke of Budget smiled. They both agreed. Duke of Budget told Baby Bird Budget, "Inhale and exhale three times before you answer. Listen very closely as the Count tells you the story."

Baby Bird Budget inhaled and exhaled three times. "I can do it! I can do it! I know I can do it!" She patted herself on the top of her head and hugged herself tightly until tears filled her eyes.

The Count began to tell the story. "You have a very lovely board game. I own an exceptionally large ship. I invite the cowboys and Indians to come aboard my ship. The cowboys carry guns. The Indians carry bows. What else do they carry? The row that begins with Start should have how many of the blank on both sides of the board game?"

Baby Bird Budget improved her board game. She wrote the answer down arrows. She drew a total of twelve arrows, six on one side of the board game and six on the other side of the board game right below the row that began with Start. She drew another twelve arrows, six on one side of the board game and six on the other side of the board game.

"I have a total of twenty-four arrows because six arrows on each side times four is twenty-four." She crossed her fingers and said, "I am not sure if I would like to add arrows."

The Count asked to see her board game. He applauded. "The board game is excellent."

Duke of Budget looked at the board game, applauded, and smiled. "Great job! Ask the Count to give you a letter of recommendation and give him your banana-colored pen."

After he signed, she gave him a banana bamboo stick and a thank-you card.

Duke of Budget studied the map and set his compass to go to Georgia. Traveling for a distance, they finally reached the zoo named Georgia. There, the Count known as World Traveler was housed.

This time, Duke of Budget beat Baby Bird Budget to a nursery rhyme song. "Juggle, juggle, juggle, jump, jump, jump. Now say your name."

Baby Bird Budget jumped three times and said, "My name is Baby Bird. Now, Grandpa, juggle, juggle, juggle, jump, jump, jump. Now say your name."

Duke of Budget grinned and hugged Baby Bird tightly. Then he knocked on the Count's door three times.

The Count opened the door and said, "Hello, my friends, come right in and recline on my grassy couch." He grinned and introduced himself. "I am the Count known as World Traveler." He now handed Duke of Budget the script.

After reading the script, Duke of Budget looked at the Count and smiled. They both agreed to read Baby Bird Budget the story.

Duke of Budget told Baby Bird Budget, "Inhale and exhale three times before you answer. Listen as the Count tells you the story."

Baby Bird Budget inhaled and exhaled three times. "I can do it! I can do it! I know I can do it!" She patted herself on the top of her head and hugged herself tightly until tears filled her eyes.

The Count began to tell his story. "You have a very lovely board game. When you visit the zoo, there are animals, popcorn, peanuts, clowns, and rides. I love to juggle pins and ride a bicycle. All the children love to give me carrots and bamboo sticks. I have performed in circus acts at the following zoos: Tennessee, Mexico City, Washington, DC, San Diego, California, and Georgia. In what country did I perform my circus acts? Where do you think you should write the names of these countries on your board game in bold letters?"

Baby Bird Budget answered, "The country where you performed your circus act is the United States. I will write the United States underneath the third row named Home in bold letters."

The Count and Duke of Budget both applauded at the same time.

Duke of Budget said, "Ask the Count to give you a letter of recommendation and give him your strawberry-colored pen."

The Count signed the letter of recommendation with a grape-colored pen. She smiled and handed him a grape bamboo stick and a thank-you card.

Duke of Budget asked Baby Bird Budget, "What is the name of the next state where Panda Bears are located?"

"Well, those are the only zoos I found!" stated Baby Bird Budget.

Duke of Budget now studied the map and set his compass to go to another state that has a zoo and no Panda Bears. They traveled for a distance and reached the zoo with no Panda Bears or Red Panda Bears. Here, they agreed to rest and use the telephone conference directory in the zoo to locate the Counts housed in zoos in foreign territories. Baby Bird Budget named the 6th zoo, on her board game "Panda Bears Wanted.

Duke of Budget told Baby Bird Budget, "Read the sign on the booth located near the animal farm in the zoo, 'Free Video Calls Today.' I think this will be a great service to use to contact the Counts housed in zoos in different foreign territories."

Baby Bird Budget was confident that she could pass all the tests. But every time she thought of what Mack and his friends did, her eyes swelled with tears.

Duke of Budget and Baby Bird Budget entered the booth and found a phone directory with listings of all the zoos on her board game, a huge computer, and a printer. In the phone directory next to each zoo was a unique code they were to dial to use the free video call service.

Baby Bird Budget kissed Duke of Budget on the cheek and hugged him tightly. "Will you write me a letter of recommendation?" She gave him a lime-green pen and her notepad. He wrote her a letter of recommendation and signed it "Duke of Budget."

Hoping that one side of her board game was complete, she rewarded herself with a chocolate-, strawberry-, vanilla-, banana-, grape-, and orange-flavored bamboo sticks.

Duke of Budget ate some as well. "Yum-yum," he said and smiled.

While sitting in the booth, Duke of Budget turned the pages in the phone directory book until he found Europe. He found the Count known as Travel Agent housed at the Scotland Zoo in Europe. The other zoos in Europe that housed Panda Bears were Austria, Spain, and France. There were no Counts at these zoos.

Baby Bird Budget's eyes swelled with tears, and she began to weep. Duke of Budget wrapped his arms around her. She stopped crying.

"Remember to inhale and exhale three times before answering."

He entered the code for Scotland located in Europe, 777, and the Count known as Travel Agent appeared on the large computer screen. "Welcome, my friends, to one of Europe's many zoos. You have reached Scotland. How may I help you?"

"Thank you for such a warm greeting. My granddaughter, Baby Bird Budget, wants to enter her board game, *Panda Bears Checkers*, for review at ABC Elementary School, and we need your expertise."

"I am pleased to help you. Let me see your granddaughter's board game."

Baby Bird Budget took her board game out of her bag, unfolded it, and held it up so the Count could see the game.

"You have a very lovely board game. I belong to an elite class of Panda Bears known as Counts. We have members in several foreign territories, including Scotland, Australia, Taiwan, Beijing, Thailand, and Kobe, Japan. What would you call these territories? I will give you a hint. The first four letters are "INT'L."

Baby Bird Budget inhaled and exhaled three times. "I can do it! I can do it! I know I can do it!" She patted herself on the top of her head and hugged herself tightly until tears filled her eyes. "Are they international territories?"

"You are correct!" replied the Count.

She wrote the name "International" on the foreign two sides of the board game.

Duke of Budget hugged Baby Bird Budget and told her, "Great job."

She asked the Count, "Do you have a vanilla-colored pen? Can you write me a letter of recommendation?"

He scanned the letter on the large computer and sent it to her.

Baby Bird Budget told him, "You will receive a gift for your help."

"Goodbye! Goodbye!" Baby Bird Budget and Duke of Budget ended the call.

The second foreign zoo location was in Australia. Baby Bird Budget read the name of the zoo from her board game. Duke of Budget turned the pages in the directory phone book until he found the zoo of Australia. There, the Count known as Architecture was housed.

Baby Bird Budget's eyes swelled with tears, and she began to weep. She was worried that this time she might fail a test. Duke of Budget wrapped his arms around her. She stopped crying.

He told her, "Remember to inhale and exhale three times before answering." He then entered the code for the zoo of Australia, 555.

The Count Known as Architecture appeared on the large computer screen. "Welcome, my friends, to the zoo of Australia. How may I help you?"

"Thank you for such a warm greeting. My granddaughter, Baby Bird Budget, wants to enter her board game, *Panda Bears Checkers*, for review at ABC Elementary School, and we need your expertise."

"I am pleased to help you. Let me see your granddaughter's board game."

Baby Bird Budget took her board game out of her bag, unfolded it, and held it up so the Count could see the game.

"This symbol would really make your board game outstanding. What symbol would you like to add to your board game? I will give you a hint. This symbol is used to add. You will need to draw twenty-four."

Baby Bird Budget inhaled and exhaled three times. "I can do it! I can do it! I know I can do it!" She patted herself on the top of her head and hugged herself tightly until tears filled her eyes. She studied her board game. "I think the plus symbols would be great to add to the middle section of my board game. I will add a total of twenty-four plus symbols to the middle section of the board game."

The Count agreed and told her, "Excellent job!"

Duke of Budget hugged Baby Bird Budget. "Great job!"

Baby Bird Budget asked the Count, "Do you have a strawberry pen? Can you write me a letter of recommendation?"

He scanned the letter on the large computer and sent it to her.

Baby Bird Budget told him, "You will receive a gift for your help."

The third foreign zoo location was Taiwan. Baby Bird Budget read the name from her board game. Duke of Budget turned the pages in the directory until he founds the zoo of Taiwan. There, the Count known as Designer was housed.

Baby Bird Budget's eyes swelled with tears, and she began to weep. Duke of Budget wrapped his arms around her. She stopped crying.

He told her, "Remember to inhale and exhale three times before answering." He entered the code for the zoo of Taiwan, 444.

The Count known as Designer appeared on the large computer screen. "Welcome, my friends, to the zoo of Taiwan. How may I help you?"

"Thank you for such a warm greeting. My granddaughter, Baby Bird Budget, wants to enter her board game, *Panda Bears Checkers*, for review at ABC Elementary School, and we need your expertise."

"I am pleased to help you. Let me see your granddaughter's board game."

Baby Bird Budget took her board game out of her bag, unfolded it, and held it up so the Count could see the game.

"You have a very lovely board game. There are two players following the rules on this board game. They are playing a game of match. What is missing on your board game? Here is the hint. You can play concentration, twenty-one blackjack, and go fish. You will make twenty-four of these for your board game. Each one will represent a state or territory."

Baby Bird Budget inhaled and exhaled three times. "I can do it! I can do it! I know I can do it!" She patted herself on the top of her head and hugged herself tightly until her eyes filled with tears.

"I am missing playing cards." She made twelve cards. "Six cards represent the zoos located in the United States and my Panda Bear friends. Six cards represent the zoos located in foreign territories with my Red Panda Bear friends." She repeated the same steps for the other two sides. She made twenty-four cards.

The Count saw the cards. "Excellent job!"

Duke of Budget hugged Baby Bird Budget. "Great job!"

Baby Bird Budget asked the Count, "Do you have a chocolate pen? Can you write me a letter of recommendation?"

He scanned the letter on the large computer and sent it to her.

Baby Bird Budget told him, "You will receive a gift for your help."

"Goodbye! Goodbye!" Baby Bird Budget and Duke of Budget now ended the call.

The fourth foreign zoo location was Beijing. Baby Bird Budget read the name from her board game. Duke of Budget turned the pages in the phone directory book until he found the zoo of Beijing. There, the Count known as Carpenter was housed.

Baby Bird Budget's eyes swelled with tears. She began to weep. Duke of Budget wrapped his arms around her. She stopped crying.

He told her, "Remember to inhale and exhale three times before answering." Duke of Budget entered the code for the zoo of Beijing, 333.

The Count known as Carpenter appeared on the huge computer screen. "Welcome my friends to the zoo of Beijing. How may I help you?"

"Thank you for such a warm greeting. My granddaughter, Baby Bird Budget, wants to enter her board game, *Panda Bears Checkers*, in the contest at ABC Elementary School. We need your advice."

"I am pleased to help you. Let me see your granddaughter's board game," exclaimed the Count.

Baby Bird Budget held up the board game so the Count could see it.

"You have a very lovely board game. Imagine you are playing your board game. You will need game pieces to get across the board game. There are twenty-four zoos. How many will you need? Hint. There are four squares for each zoo."

Baby Bird Budget inhaled and exhaled three times. "I can do it! I can do it! I know I can do it!" She patted herself on the top of her head and hugged herself tightly until tears filled her eyes.

She began to count. "There are twelve zoos on two sides. There are four squares for each zoo that holds a game piece. Twelve times four equals forty-eight game pieces for two sides. A total of ninety-six squares for all four sides."

The Count smiled. "My words cannot express, what a great job. Perfect!"

Baby Bird Budget asked the Count, "Do you have a banana pen? Can you write me a letter of recommendation?"

He scanned the letter on the huge computer and sent it to her.

Duke of Budget told him, "You will receive a gift for your help."

"Goodbye! Goodbye!" Baby Bird Budget and Duke of Budget ended the call.

The fifth foreign zoo location was Thailand. Baby Bird Budget read the name from her board game. Duke of Budget turned the pages in the phone directory book until he found the zoo of Thailand. There, the Count known as Craft was housed.

Baby Bird Budget's eyes swelled with tears. She began to weep. Duke of Budget wrapped his arms around her. She stopped crying.

He told her, "Remember to inhale and exhale three times before answering." He entered the code for the zoo of Thailand, 222.

The Count known as Craft appeared on the large computer screen. "Welcome, my friends, to the zoo of Thailand. How may I help you?"

"Thank you for such a warm greeting. My granddaughter, Baby Bird Budget, wants to enter her board game, *Panda Bears Checkers*, in a contest at ABC Elementary School. We need your help."

"I am pleased to help you. Let me see the board game."

Baby Bird Budget held up the board game so the Count could see the game.

"You have a very lovely board game. You need to improve your dice. You have four dice. The Panda Bears are on one die, and the Red Panda Bears are on the other. You need to number these dice."

Baby Bird Budget inhaled and exhaled three times. "I can do it! I can do it! I know I can do it!" She patted herself on the top of her head and hugged herself tightly until tears filled her eyes.

She picked up her Panda Bears and Red Panda Bears die. She wrote on the Panda Bears die a number from one through five and "Panda Bear Wanted." The Red Panda Bears die was numbered from one to six.

The Count congratulated Baby Bird Budget. "Great job!"

Baby Bird Budget asked the Count, "Do you have a grape pen? Can you write me a letter of recommendation to take to ABC Elementary School?"

He scanned the letter on the computer and sent it to her.

Duke of Budget told him, "You will receive a gift for your help."

"Goodbye! Goodbye!" Baby Bird Budget and Duke of Budget ended the call.

The sixth foreign zoo location was Kobe, Japan. Baby Bird Budget read the name from her board game. Duke of Budget turned the pages in the phone directory book until he found the zoo of Kobe, Japan. There, the Count known as Merchant was housed.

Baby Bird Budget's eyes swelled with tears. She began to weep. Duke of Budget wrapped his arms around her. She stopped crying.

He told her, "Remember to inhale and exhale three times before answering." He entered the code for the zoo of Kobe, Japan, 111.

The Count known as Merchant appeared on the large computer screen. "Welcome, my friends, to the zoo of Kobe, Japan. How may I help you?"

"Thank you for such a warm greeting. My granddaughter, Baby Bird Budget, wants to enter her board game, *Panda Bears Checkers*, in a contest at ABC Elementary School. We need your help."

"I am pleased to help you. Let me see your granddaughter's board game."

Baby Bird Budget held up the board game so the Count could see the game. Surprisingly, she had suddenly stopped weeping.

"You have a very lovely board game. Your board game is missing the title. What is its title?"

Baby Bird Budget inhaled and exhaled three times. "I can do it! I can do it! I know I can do it!" She patted herself on the top of her head and hugged herself tightly until tears filled her eyes.

"The title of my board game is *Panda Bears Checkers.*" She wrote the title of the board game in bold letters in the middle section of the board game. Next, she wrote the title on the side of her board game. She drew the Panda Bear, Red Panda Bear, two spinning wheels numbered one through six, and two spinning wheels with all twelve zoos on both spinning wheels.

The Count congratulated Baby Bird Budget. "Great job!"

Baby Bird Budget asked the Count, "Do you have an orange-colored pen? Can you write me a letter of recommendation?"

He scanned the letter on the large computer screen and sent it to her.

Duke of Budget told him, "You will receive a gift for your help."

"Goodbye! Goodbye!" Baby Bird Budget and Duke of Budget ended the call.

"Grandpa, I am impressed with my new board game. The Counts' questions were not too hard. Thank you for helping me to relax, Grandpa."

Duke of Budget now extended his arms and said, "Congratulations, you are now the winner of your board game. Let us test the game and see how long it takes to play *Panda Bears Checkers.*"

Baby Bird Budget hugged him. "Thank you, Grandpa. I really enjoyed the trips."

Duke of Budget set the timer on his watch. "Wow! You won the game, Baby Bird Budget. You got all your Panda Bear game pieces home first. The game takes at least one hour to play. The journey is over. We now can return home."

Baby Bird Budget gathered all eleven letters of recommendation, the board game, playing cards, four dice, ninety-six game pieces, five pens, a notepad, and the remainder of her candy bamboo sticks. She packed them in her bag.

They now left the zoo called Panda Bears Wanted. They traveled through the mountains until they arrived home.

The trip was not quite over. On the way home, a powerful Panda Bear ruler would rant and rave every time the children would bring him inventions for approval. With his stamp of approval, they were sure to surpass the teachers' remarks. But because of his cruel disposition, the children would dare not let him see their new toys, baby dolls, and board game inventions.

But one little Panda Bear named Sneaky was willing to take a chance to get Baby Bird Budget the "A" prize. He knew the Ruler of the land would make her or break her strategy for success.

"Hey!" Sneaky screamed at the top of his lungs. "I searched for you every day through the mountain trail." He joined Duke of Budget and Baby Bird Budget on the way home. "How was your trip?"

"I won all the challenges and was able to complete my board game. Would you like to see it?" asked Baby Bird Budget.

"Hurry up," said Sneaky, "and show me your board game."

"We will meet the powerful landlord," said Baby Bird Budget.

Sneaky Panda replied, "Ok enough! Hurry!" "We are going to meet this powerful landlord."

Baby Bird Budget smiled somewhat as she stared at her board game, mustering the courage to present the game to this ruler. She folded the game and placed it in the bag.

They raced across seven mountainsides and through murky water to reach the castle. Once they arrived, Baby Bird Budget started panting heavily, and her eyes began to water. She had forgotten what her grandpa had taught her about overcoming fear.

Sneaky observed that she was emotional and whispered his ancient hidden secret in her ear. She giggled and laughed. She convinced herself that she could conquer any challenge.

Sneaky knocked on the castle door three times. Knock! Knock! Knock!

An elderly Panda Bear opened the door and stared at them sternly. "Yes, how may I help you?"

Sneaky replied, "My best friend Baby Bird Budget has successfully completed her board game, and we would like your honest opinion."

The landlord's temper became extremely hot, and his voice reached a crescendo as he screamed out, "Throw these two trespassers into detention."

The guards grabbed Sneaky and immediately forced him to the ground.

Baby Bird Budget screamed as loud as she can, "You are my great-grandfather. How could you?"

The landlord's face became cold as stone. For several weeks he stood in the doorway with the same facial expression. To this day, the Red Panda Bears and Black Panda Bears visit an exceedingly kind ruler that waves from the steeple of his castle.

After the long journey, Baby Bird Budget hugged Sneaky and said goodbye. She was so excited about her new and improved board game that she walked into her house and right by her parents and forgot to speak.

Mama Budget grabbed her and hugged her tightly. Papa Budget said, "We missed you." Wu Budget asked, "Did you answer all the Counts' questions correctly?"

Baby Bird Budget said, "Yes."

"Great!" They all applauded. "The board game will be a success!"

Wu Budget told Baby Bird Budget, "Tomorrow is the day of the contest at ABC Elementary School. Are you ready?"

Baby Bird Budget agreed. "I am ready!"

The next day arrived. All the students and Baby Bird Budget rehearsed their presentations and signed up their toy inventions. All the Panda Bear parents, including Duke of Budget, Papa Budget, Mama Budget, and Wu Budget, were seated in the classroom to see and learn about all the new toy inventions. Many of the students re-entered the same toy/game invention.

Mack re-entered his race car that had placed first in last month's competition. The audience was impressed with his presentation. They all applauded.

Finally, the judges called the last competitor, Baby Bird Budget, to present her board game invention. Baby Bird Budget felt she had overcome her fears and could share her experience. She was so happy that her family sat in the first row in the classroom that she could not stop smiling.

"My grandfather, Duke of Budget, and I had the opportunity to travel and meet the most intelligent Panda Bears in the world, the Counts. I personally learned how to build my confidence to be creative. But most importantly, I thank my grandfather, who helped me to overcome low self-esteem and to think. Here is my board game, *Panda Bears Checkers*, better known as *A Panda Bear Board Game.*"

She showed the audience her board game. They all applauded. The audience loved the board game and her presentation so much that they stood and continued to applaud.

Afterward the judges ranked the new toy inventions. Mack's sophisticated car placed second. Baby Bird Budget's board game, *Panda Bears Checkers*, placed first with a stamp of approval from the ruler of the land, her great-grandfather.

Baby Bird Budget's parents and Duke of Budget embraced her with kisses.

She whispered in Duke of Budget's ear, "Did you remember to send the candy-flavored bamboo sticks and the thank-you cards?"

"Yes, I did," replied Duke of Budget.

Mack now approached Baby Bird Budget. "Congratulations, you are now welcome to join the "A" list of students at ABC Elementary School."

"Hey, Mack, you are still too proud to apologize for your behavior. I have many friends, and you are not one."

About the Author

Michelle Sheree Andrews is the author behind *A PANDA BEAR'S BOARD GAME*. She is a Medical Assistant and fiction writer. One of her best contributions in a lifetime, is as a Senior in high school, she worked for Stockton State Hospital Summer Program. The hospital is where she performed Nursing Aide duties, caring for children and adults with disabilities. A favorite pastime, was to read stories and sing nursery rhymes to a niece with this disorder.

In memory of her creative and loving mom, Opal Randolph, she attributes most of her success as a writer and storybook builder.

Lightning Source UK Ltd.
Milton Keynes UK
UKHW052137090820
367889UK00002B/38